A MEDAL
—FOR—
MALINA

by

NARINDER DHAMI

Illustrated by Kate Rogers

HAMISH HAMILTON
LONDON

For my mother and father

HAMISH HAMILTON LTD
Published by the Penguin Group
27 Wrights Lane, London W8 5TZ, England
Viking Penguin Inc., 40 West 23rd Street, New York, New York 10010, USA
Penguin Books Australia Ltd, Ringwood, Victoria, Australia
Penguin Books Canada Ltd, 2801 John Street, Markham, Ontario, Canada L3R 1B4
Penguin Books (NZ) Ltd, 182–190 Wairau Road, Auckland 10, New Zealand

Penguin Books Ltd, Registered Offices: Harmondsworth, Middlesex, England

First published in Great Britain by Hamish Hamilton Ltd 1990

Text copyright © 1990 by Narinder Dhami
Text illustrations copyright © 1990 by Kate Rogers
1 3 5 7 9 10 8 6 4 2

A CIP catalogue record for this book is available from the British Library

ISBN 0-241-12937-0

Typeset in Linotron Baskerville by Rowland Phototypesetting (London) Ltd
Printed in Great Britain at the University Press, Cambridge

Chapter One

JOHN PARRY WAS charging round the playground annoying the girls again. First he'd kicked Malina's ball away into the prickly bushes outside the caretaker's house. Malina and Katy had had to get down on their hands and knees and crawl through the dirt to get the ball back. Then he'd sneaked up behind Charlene, and pinched her bottom. Katy and Charlene had tried chasing him, but they had given up. John was just too fast for them.

"Get lost, John Parry, or we'll tell Miss Sharma," said Malina crossly.

1

John was standing just out of reach, his ginger hair flopping over one eye, sticking his tongue out at them.

"Oooh, I'm really frightened!" he crowed scornfully. He moved a little bit closer. "Just 'cos you can't catch me yourselves –"

Katy suddenly rushed forward, her blonde pony-tail swinging furiously from side to side, and made a quick grab at John. But she only caught at the air. John was too fast for her. He leapt backwards, hooting with laughter.

"You're wasting your time!" he shouted. "Girls can't run as fast as boys – it's a well-known fact!"

"Oh, change the record, John Parry!" said Malina.

"I beat you in the Maths test this morning, so there," said Charlene.

"I'm talking about running!"

shouted John. "Who cares about *Maths*?"

The three girls turned their backs on him, but that was a big mistake. Next second, John had pulled Malina's red ribbon off one of her long black plaits, and sent it fluttering across the playground on the wind. Malina raced after it, and caught it just before it sailed out of the gate.

"I'm sick of that stupid wally," Malina grumbled as she came back. "I wish we could lock him in the boys' toilets or something."

"And stick his head down the loo and pull the chain!" Katy grinned.

"Except his head's so big, it wouldn't fit!" Charlene giggled.

"There's just one problem – we'd have to catch him first," said Malina.

"You might be able to catch him, Malina. You're fast," said Charlene.

"Now wait a minute –" Malina began.

"Yes, go on, Malina!" said Katy eagerly. "He might leave us alone then."

Malina felt a little bit uncomfortable. She knew she could beat any girl in the school. She was tall and thin and she had long legs. Her dad had said that if

she grew any taller she wouldn't be able to get through the front door. But John Parry was still just a little bit bigger than she was. And if she chased him, and he got away from her, she'd never hear the end of it. He had the biggest motormouth in the whole school. But . . . it was worth a try. Wasn't it?

Malina looked round. John Bigmouth Parry was standing right behind them. She fixed her eyes on his red sweater. She took one tiny step towards him.

John just stood and watched. Malina knew that he knew what she was going to do. And by the big grin on his stupid face, she knew that he thought it was a good joke. She took another step towards him. And another. And then John turned and ran like the wind across the playground.

Malina followed. She broke into a run, her arms and legs beginning to work hard as she built up speed, her eyes fixed on John's red sweater in front of her. She was not going to let him get away this time she told herself fiercely.

John ran past the caretaker's house, and past the teachers' cars, knocking over a couple of first years on the way. Malina followed. Then he veered sharply to the left and disappeared round the back of the school. They'd been told in assembly yesterday that they were to keep away from there because there were builders working on the roof, but Malina didn't stop to think about *that*. The wind had begun to burn her throat and sting her ears, but she knew she had to keep going.

Next second they were back in the playground, and John was racing

towards the dinner hall with Malina
hot on his heels. Was it just her
imagination – or was she getting just a
little tiny bit nearer to that red blur in
front of her?

John ran right through a game of
football. Malina was right behind him.

Someone yelled at them to get out of the way, but they took no notice. John was only a couple of yards in front of Malina now, and she could hear him panting hard. The lesson bell rang out, but Malina didn't hear it with the wind whistling in her ears and the sound of her heart thumping.

Now John was running straight towards the school office. He wouldn't dare to run inside, surely . . . He'd swerve away from the door at the last minute. Bighead John Parry trying to be clever, Malina thought. Well, she'd be ready for him. She was so close behind him now that she could almost reach out and touch his sweater. She stretched out her hand – just a bit more – her fingers touched soft red wool – SHE'D GOT HIM –

"OWWWW!"

"AAAARGH!"

The Headmaster stepped out of the office and into the path of John Parry. To her horror, Malina couldn't stop herself in time. She flew forward like an arrow and head-butted Mr Collins right in the middle of his large stomach.

"JOHN – PARRY! MALINA – PATEL!" Mr Collins was gasping for air like a whale out of water. "MY – OFFICE! IMMEDIATELY!"

Chapter Two

WHEN CLASS FIVE lined up for dinner later that morning, Malina made sure she kept well out of John's way. He was at the front of the dinner queue as usual, talking at the top of his voice and cheeking the dinner ladies. Because of that bigmouth, Malina thought gloomily, she'd ended up with two detentions from the Headmaster and a telling-off from her own teacher, Miss Sharma. John Parry was trouble with a capital T – and from now on she was going to pretend he *didn't even exist*.

"You did catch him though,

Malina," said Katy.

"So what?" grumbled Malina. "It didn't do me any good, did it? What's for dinner?"

"Sausages or cheese pie," said Charlene, looking over all the heads in front of them. "Cabbage, carrots and peas."

"I hate cabbage almost as much as I hate John Parry," said Malina crossly. "And I'm never, ever going to speak to him again as long as I live!"

Katy and Charlene looked at each other. Then they both looked at Malina.

"What's the matter with you two?" Malina asked, frowning.

"You tell her, Charlene," said Katy.

"Well," Charlene began carefully. "You know that it's Sports Day next week . . ."

"Yes," said Malina. "So?"

"We want you to thrash John Parry in the sixty metre sprint!" Katy shouted.

Malina's mouth fell open.

"You're mad!" she gasped. "You know he beat me last year!"

"But you're faster now!" Charlene

17

argued. "Anyway, you could train –"

"NO!" said Malina. "I don't even want to *think* about him."

"Oh Malina!" wailed Katy. "Don't you remember what he was like when he won last year?"

"You could beat him, Malina!" Charlene said eagerly. "You could win the gold medal!"

"I'm not racing against John Parry ANY MORE," said Malina. "This year I'm going to enter the sack race or the skipping race. Not the sprint."

Charlene and Katy's faces fell.

"That means John's going to win the gold medal again," sighed Charlene.

"And he'll wear it on a string round his neck for the rest of term," said Katy gloomily.

"Oh – all right!" snapped Malina. She couldn't let her friends down, could

18

19

20

she? And maybe – a tiny little flame of hope flickered up inside her – maybe she could beat him after all? "I'll do it!"

"Brilliant!" shouted Katy.

"But you've got to train hard," said Charlene sternly. "Lots of running practice – and you've got to eat the right food –"

"And that means lots of greens!" added Katy.

"Oh well, at least there's apple pie for afters," sighed Malina.

"And no puddings!" said Charlene firmly.

After dinner Malina sat on the playground wall, her chin in her hands. She could see John Parry playing football in front of her. He'd just tackled someone for the ball – or rather, he'd just pushed one of the other players over. None of the children had said anything though – they were all too frightened of him. Malina watched John dribble the ball towards the goal and score, and her heart sank. Maybe she'd just been lucky when she was chasing John today. Perhaps she didn't have a chance of beating him at Sports Day after all . . . Maybe she should tell Charlene and Katy that she'd changed her mind.

Malina got up, and went slowly into school to change into her trainers. She'd promised her friends that she'd start practising right away, but the more she thought about it, the more her heart was sinking into her shoes. As Malina went into the cloakroom, she couldn't help noticing a plastic bag hanging on the very first coat peg. 'This is John Parry's peg – so WATCH OUT!!!' was scrawled across the bag in

This is
John Parry's
peg
-so WATCH
OUT

felt tip pen. Malina stood and stared at the bag for a few minutes, frowning. It was time that boy was taught a lesson – and she was the only person in the school who had a chance to do it . . .

Charlene and Katy were waiting for her outside.

"Come on, we'd better start your training!" Katy called.

"*We?*" said Malina. "I thought I was the one who had to beat John Parry?"

"We're going to help you," said Charlene. "Look." She was wearing a large white stopwatch on a cord around her neck. "Miss Sharma lent it to me."

"What for?"

"Run round the playground and I'll time you," said Charlene importantly. "Then tomorrow we'll see if you can go any faster."

"On your marks!" shouted Katy.

"Come on, Malina!"

"Okay, okay," said Malina crossly.
She wasn't quite sure how running
round the playground every day was
going to help her beat John Parry next
week, but she'd try anything.

"GO!"

Malina set off. It was odd just running, and she felt a bit embarrassed. There was no one to chase or race. As she set off some of the other children shouted something rude and two of them even tried to run after her and catch her, but Malina beat them easily. She imagined she was running in the

sprint race and that made her speed up. She felt strong and smooth, fast and graceful.

Charlene hit the button on the stopwatch as Malina skidded to a halt, panting her head off.

"Fifty-five seconds!" she said. "Owwwww!"

John Parry had sneaked up behind them to see what they were doing and had grabbed a handful of Charlene's tiny plaits.

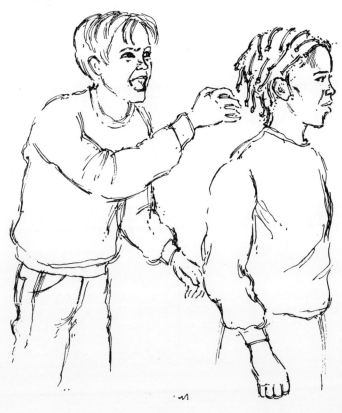

"You pest!" shouted Charlene furiously, rubbing her head. "Why can't you mind your own business!"

John grinned annoyingly. "What're you lot doing? You might as well tell me because I'll find out anyway."

"If you must know, bighead," said Katy, "Malina's going to beat you in the sprint next week!"

"Ssshh!" hissed Malina. "I didn't want anyone to know!"

But it was too late. Some of the other children in their class had already begun to drift over to find out what was going on.

"Look, John, she's in training," said one of the boys. "You'd better start too."

John started to laugh. "You're joking! Train to beat a stupid girl?"

"Well, *we're* not joking!" snapped

Charlene. "Malina's going to make you look like a real fool, aren't you, Malina? Malina! Where are you going?"

"To the toilet – I feel sick!" gulped Malina. "It must be all that cabbage you made me eat!"

When Malina got home that night, she couldn't wait to tell everybody what was happening.

"I'm in training!" she told her mum proudly.

"For what?" asked Mum. She was feeding Ajay, Malina's baby brother, before she went off to work.

"Sports Day," Malina said. "I'm going to win the gold medal in the sprint."

Mum shook her head. "Never mind gold medals," she said. "How was your spelling test?"

32

"Oh, *that*," said Malina. "Nine out of ten. I got 'receive' wrong."

Mum sighed. "You'd better think less about your running, and more about your schoolwork, Malina. Now take this cup of tea in to your dad."

Malina edged her way carefully into the shop next door to the house, trying not to spill a single drop of tea on the way. Dad was wrapping up some carrots for Mrs Jones, who lived just down the road, so Malina put the tea on the counter and sat down on a bag of chapatti flour. Mrs Jones never stopped talking, but Dad always said he didn't mind, because she only had her cat, Smoky, to talk to at home. Malina usually didn't mind either, but tonight she couldn't wait for Mrs Jones to go.

"I'm in training!" she burst out as soon as Mrs Jones had one foot out of the door.

"Training?" Her dad looked surprised.

"I'm going to win the sprint at Sports Day," said Malina importantly.

Dad sipped his cup of tea.

"I used to win all the running competitions when I was your age." He smiled at Malina. "Nobody can beat us Patels!"

Malina giggled. Dad was so round and fat now, she couldn't imagine him ever running anywhere. Dad wagged his finger at her.

"Oh, yes! I was fast. I could have been in the Olympics!"

"I only want to beat John Parry," Malina explained.

"Beat John Parry – and then go to the Olympics!" chuckled Dad. "Why not?"

Malina closed her eyes, and
imagined herself winning a gold medal
at the Olympic games. She'd seen it on
the telly – the winner standing on a
little platform, being presented with
flowers and a gold medal. And then
they played the National Anthem and
everybody cried. Maybe, one day, it'd
be *her* standing on the platform with a

gold medal round her neck. But she soon came back down to earth with a bump – first she had to beat Bigmouth Parry. And that was *exactly* what she was going to do.

Chapter Three

THE NEXT DAY EVERYONE at school was talking about Malina, John and Sports Day. It looked like almost everyone wanted to see John get beaten next week. By the time Class Five went out for rounders practice that afternoon, Malina was feeling pretty pleased with herself. And she'd run round the playground three seconds faster than yesterday. Charlene and Katy were sure she was going to beat the pants off John Parry next week. They couldn't stop talking about it.

"Right, Class Five!" called Miss

Sharma. "Shall we begin?"

Class Five stopped talking. It was best not to muck around with Miss Sharma. It was a warm, sunny day and no one wanted to get sent inside to write

a story or something instead of playing rounders.

"Right, two teams," Miss Sharma said briskly. "No, stay where you are; I'll choose the teams, thank you." A few children moaned under their breath, but Miss Sharma didn't take a scrap of notice.

Malina was put in the same team as John Parry, and their team lined up to bat first.

"Trust me to get stuck in the same team as a deadhead like *you*!" said John immediately. "How's your training going then?"

"Okay, thank you," said Malina.

"You're wasting your time," said John rudely. "You'll never beat me in a trillion years." He pushed his way in front of Malina. "Anyway, I was here before you, for a start!"

Malina made a face at the back of John's head. She wasn't going to argue with him. She was just going to beat him in the sprint next week. That should shut him up once and for all!

Malina made two rounders before she was out. John was out first ball, which put him in an evil mood.

"Stay right out of my way, Malina Patel," John muttered, when it was their team's turn to field. "I don't want you taking any of my catches."

Malina and John were both fielding near second base, but Malina moved as far away from him as she could. What a revolting boy he was! She was really beginning to look forward to Sports Day.

It was Charlene's turn to bat. She was a strong hitter, and she whacked the ball high up into the air. It sailed

over second base and began to dip
down towards Malina. Malina ran
backwards, keeping her eye on the ball.
She could probably catch it – as long as
she was careful –

Suddenly someone gave Malina a giant thump. The force sent her flying. She tumbled head first onto the grass, a sharp pain running up her leg from her ankle. The ball bounced away and rolled to a stop.

"John Parry!" shouted Miss Sharma, running towards them. "What on earth were you doing? That was Malina Patel's catch!"

John untangled his arms and legs from Malina's, and sat up, rubbing the side of his head. His shorts were covered in grass stains.

"I thought she'd miss it," he mumbled, "so I went for it."

"Are you all right, Malina?" Charlene asked, looking worried. Both teams had come running over, and were standing around Malina and John.

Malina nodded. But when she tried

to stand up, she began to cry.

"My ankle! It really hurts!"

Miss Sharma knelt down on the grass, and gently felt Malina's foot.

"I don't think it's broken," she said. "But it could be sprained. Katy, run and find Mr Collins, and tell him what's happened."

Malina still couldn't put any weight on her foot, so the Headmaster carried her to Miss Sharma's car. Then Miss Sharma drove Malina home. Malina cried all the way there. When they arrived, her dad had to carry Malina upstairs and put her to bed. Dad fetched Mum from the shop. Malina only stopped crying when Doctor Singh came to see her, and that was because her eyes were too sore to cry any more.

"It's quite a bad sprain," Doctor Singh said, when he'd had a good look at Malina's foot. "She must rest it for a week, and the swelling should go down."

"A week!" gasped Malina. "What about Sports Day?"

"Thank you, Doctor Singh," said Mrs Patel as he got up to leave.

"What about Sports Day?" wailed Malina. Her mum gave her a look which said 'be quiet or else'. Malina kept quiet, but she couldn't stop one last, fat tear squeezing itself out of one eye. She wouldn't be going to Sports Day; she wouldn't be getting the gold medal; and Bigmouth John Parry would be boasting about it all over the place. She'd never live it down. Never.

Charlene and Katy came round to see Malina after school.

"Hello, Malina," said Charlene cheerfully.

"We've brought you some comics," smiled Katy.

"Why are you two looking so happy?" Malina said crossly. "I'm missing Sports Day, and guess who's

46

going to win that gold medal?!"

Charlene and Katy looked uneasy.

"We know," said Charlene. "But your mum told us not to talk about Sports Day."

"In case you start feeling miserable," Katy added.

"I'm miserable already," Malina sighed. "Maybe someone else will beat John Parry next week."

"Yes, maybe," agreed Charlene and Katy.

But secretly they all knew that nobody in the whole school could – except Malina. John was going to win that gold medal, and that's all there was to it.

Chapter Four

THE NEXT FEW DAYS were the most
boring of Malina's life. She had to lie
still in bed, and she wasn't allowed to
move except to go to the toilet.
Charlene and Katy came round to visit
her a few times, but seeing them made
Malina feel worse. All she could think
about was John Parry with the gold
medal round his neck.

On Tuesday, the day before Sports
Day, her dad carried Malina into the
shop and sat her in a chair near the
window so that she could look out into
the street. She watched the cars go by

51

for a while, and then began to tidy the shelves. They didn't really need tidying, but she couldn't think of anything else to do. She was bored with jigsaws and puzzles and reading and colouring.

"Shall I fetch your colouring book, Malina?" asked Dad. He was filling the shop freezer with bags of frozen vegetables.

"No thanks, Dad," sighed Malina. "I think my fingers will drop off if I colour any more pictures."

"Never mind," said Dad. "In a few days you'll be running about again."

"But not in time for Sports Day," Malina grumbled. She was trying to be cheerful, but it was difficult. The silly thing was, her ankle didn't feel too bad – not half as bad as a few days ago. Perhaps she'd even try standing up on it today . . .

"I'm going into the yard to get some more vegetables," said Dad. "If any customers come in, tell them I'll only be a few minutes."

"Okay, Dad." Malina carried on tidying the shelves until he'd gone out, then she stretched out her bandaged ankle in front of her and began to wiggle it cautiously from side to side. It hardly hurt at all. Maybe she should try standing up on it. If she could stand without too much pain, then maybe – just maybe – there was still a chance to win the gold medal. Slowly she began to haul herself out of the chair –

"Hello, dear." The door opened and Mrs Jones came into the shop. She smiled at Malina. "How are you feeling today?"

"Much better!" said Malina

breathlessly. She stood up very very carefully, putting her injured foot slowly on the ground. There was a slight twinge of pain, but it wasn't too bad. "Can I help you?"

"Are you sure you should be standing up, dear?" said Mrs Jones, frowning. "I thought your father said you had to rest it for a week?"

"I'm fine, Mrs Jones, really!" Malina hobbled triumphantly across to the counter, trying to ignore the nagging ache in her leg. "What can I get you?"

"Malina!" Dad came in from the yard carrying a pile of boxes, but he almost dropped them all on the floor when he saw Malina behind the counter. "What are you doing?"

"My ankle's a lot better, Dad!" said Malina eagerly. "I just wanted to try it out."

"The doctor said you had to rest it for a week – and that's exactly what you're going to do." Dad hurried over to the counter, picked up Malina and put her back in the chair. "You'll be telling me next you're fit enough to go to Sports Day tomorrow!"

"Well –" said Malina hopefully.

"NO!" said Dad.

The next day was Wednesday. Sports Day. Malina sat in the living-room, and wished for the 565th time that she was at school. She'd never wanted to be at school so much in her life! There was a pile of comics next to her, but she didn't feel like reading. She'd been watching a video, but all those people running about and singing happily had made her feel worse.

Mum came in with Malina's lunch on a tray. Chicken curry, chapattis, and two whole poppadoms! But Malina couldn't eat a thing. She pulled bits off the chapatti and rolled them around in her fingers. Mum saw what she was doing, but she didn't say anything.

Everyone would be getting ready now, Malina thought. And everyone would be talking in excited voices, wondering who was going to win the sack race, the egg and spoon race, the skipping race . . . Her ankle felt so much better, she was sure she could still run in the race this afternoon. But Mum had taken the day off work today to stay with Malina, so she didn't even have a chance of sneaking out. Right now John Parry was probably running round the classroom, all dressed up in his sports kit, telling everyone he was going to win the gold medal.

"Malina?"

"Yes, Mum?"

"Your dad has to go out for half an hour, so I have to look after the shop." Mum picked Ajay up, and balanced him on her hip. Malina's heart jumped. Was this going to be her chance after all? "I won't be gone for long."

Malina managed to keep calm until Mum and Ajay had gone out of the room, but then a big grin spread across her face. Half an hour was all she needed to get dressed in her shorts and trainers and get to school. Mum and Dad would be furious when they found out she'd gone – but at least she'd have the gold medal. And she was sure her ankle wouldn't *really* hurt at all –

"Oww!" Malina stood up quickly, and winced a little as her foot touched the ground. However much she tried to ignore it, her ankle was still a little bit painful. But what could she do about it?

Suddenly Malina had a brilliant idea. It was so brilliant she hopped around the room with delight. It would be easy, too. Mum was in the shop and Dad had gone out.

Malina hobbled straight into the kitchen picking up a towel on the way, and unlocked the back door. She didn't

have any shoes on, and there was no
time to go back for them, so she went up
the path to the shed on her bare feet.

In one corner of the shed was a large freezer. Dad used it to store packets of frozen food before he put them into the shop. Malina found an old wooden crate and climbed onto it. The freezer lid was heavy and hard to lift. But Malina managed it.

Cold, frosty air steamed out. Malina looked inside. The freezer was packed with bags of vegetables. Malina took out a couple of large bags of peas, and then closed the lid. She sat down on the box, and carefully wrapped the towel around her bandaged ankle. Then she took a deep breath, and stuck the frozen bags on her foot.

For a few seconds Malina couldn't feel anything. Then she began to feel the icy cold biting through to her bones. Malina gasped and shivered. I just hope this works, she said to herself over and over again. It was her only chance.

After a minute or two, Malina couldn't feel her foot at all. She took off the frozen bags, and stamped her feet carefully up and down a few times. Her ankle still ached a little, but not enough to stop her from running. And she had just enough time left to change and get to school for Sports Day.

John Bighead Parry was in for a real surprise!

Chapter Five

BY THE TIME Malina got to school everyone was already out on the field, waiting for Sports Day to begin.

"Malina!" Charlene and Katy saw her and began waving. Malina hurried over to them.

"My foot's better!" she called. "I can run after all!"

"Brilliant!" shouted Charlene.

"Oooh, I must go and tell John Parry!" said Katy happily. "He's going to be so-o-o mad!" And she ran off to look for him.

"Malina!" Miss Sharma came over,

carrying a clipboard. "What are you doing here? Have you come to watch?"

"No, Miss – I've come to run!" said Malina.

"Run?"

"Please, Miss!" begged Malina.

"Well," said Miss Sharma. "If you're sure you're all right?"

"I am, I am!" said Malina. And it was true. Almost. Her ankle wasn't hurting *too* much. Miss Sharma smiled.

"I'll put you down for the sprint then," she said. "Good luck!"

Katy came running back, looking very pleased with herself.

"John Parry is MAD!" she announced with a big smile.

"Serves him right," said Charlene. "He's been boasting all week about winning the gold medal."

"Third Year Sack Race!" called Miss

Sharma.

"That's me!" squealed Katy. "Wish me luck!"

Malina and Charlene found a place to sit down by the finishing line. There were mums and dads and other people who'd come along to watch and everyone was chattering excitedly. Children were running to and fro and the teachers were scurrying after them, trying to round them up, so that they could start the first race. It was a hot, sunny afternoon, and there wasn't a cloud to be seen in the clear, blue sky. The teachers had decorated the trees with rows and rows of coloured flags that fluttered gently in the slight breeze.

Malina felt excited and sad at the same time. She wished *her* mum and dad could be there to see her run. She'd left a note for her mum saying she'd

gone to school, but she was going to be
in big trouble when she went home
again. Still, she didn't care about that –
as long as she had the gold medal!

Charlene nudged Malina, and
pointed to the starting line.

"The Sack Race is about to start."

"Come on, Katy!" yelled Malina.

They watched Katy line up with ten other third years for the Sack Race. The sacks were laid out on the floor and as soon as Miss Sharma called 'GO!' the children had to get into them and jump to the finishing-line. But Katy got tangled up in her sack straightaway and fell over. She was last. Malina laughed

until her sides ached.

"Never mind, Katy," said Charlene after the race. "You're still in the Egg and Spoon."

"I bet I make a mess of that, too!" Katy grumbled.

They watched a few of the Lower School races, then Miss Sharma called out 'Third Year Egg and Spoon!' and Katy and Charlene went off. Malina was left on her own. She could see John Parry standing talking to some of his mates up near the starting line. He was probably boasting about how easily he was going to win the gold medal, Malina thought grimly. But she was going to make sure he didn't.

Charlene's mum and dad and her older brother were sitting near Malina, and they all started to cheer loudly for Charlene when the Egg and Spoon

Race started. Charlene was the only
one who didn't drop her china egg once,
and she won easily. Katy was last
again. Her egg rolled off her spoon and
right across the track and one of the
other children in the race tripped over it
and got a nosebleed.

"I won! I won!" Charlene shouted, running up to Malina after the race. Katy was following her, looking a bit miserable.

"I'm going to be the only one of us who doesn't win a gold medal!" she grumbled. "Charlene's won the Egg and Spoon, and Malina's going to win the sprint –"

"I haven't won yet," Malina said quietly. Her ankle was beginning to feel a bit more painful, but she couldn't tell Charlene and Katy that.

"You will!" said Katy confidently. "Maybe Miss Sharma will let me have a go at the Potato Grab. I'll go and ask her."

"Malina?" said Charlene, frowning, as Katy ran off. "Are you sure you're going to be all right?"

"'Course I am!" answered Malina as

cheerfully as she could. She couldn't
give up now – could she?

They watched Katy line up for the
Potato Grab. Malina was beginning to
feel a little bit sick inside. After the
Potato Grab, there was the Skipping
Race – and then – and then – if *only* her
ankle didn't let her down –

"Malina!" Excitedly Charlene
clutched Malina's arm. "Katy's
winning!"

The children taking part in the
Potato Grab had to take potatoes from
one bucket to another, and then to run
with the full bucket to the finishing-line.
Katy was doing well, and she'd almost
filled her bucket.

"Come on, Katy!" screamed Malina
and Charlene together.

Red in the face, Katy staggered for
the finishing-line with the heavy

bucket, crossed it first, and collapsed in a heap. Malina and Charlene leapt to their feet, cheering, but immediately Malina felt an extra-sharp twinge of pain shoot up her leg. She looked at Charlene quickly, hoping that she hadn't noticed. Charlene hadn't. She was too busy congratulating Katy, who danced over to them, beaming all over her face.

"Now we're all going to have a gold medal!" Katy crowed triumphantly. Malina felt even more sick, but she tried to force a smile. Soon she'd be lining up at the start of the sixty-metre sprint – and she had to beat John Parry. She had to . . .

Charlene went off to get some orange juice. Then they watched some of the smaller children's races, then it was the Skipping Race – and after that –

"Third Year Sprint!" called Miss Sharma.

Malina's tummy did a back-flip. Charlene and Katy looked at her solemnly.

"Good luck!" they said.

Slowly Malina got up. Her ankle still hurt, but she'd just have to put up with it. She took a deep breath, and headed for the starting-line.

John Parry had already lined up with the other runners by the time Malina got there.

"You should have stayed in bed, Malina Patel," he said cockily. "I'm going to win this race."

"We'll see about *that*!" thought Malina. She gave John a sweet smile. "Why don't you save your breath for running?" she asked. "You're going to need it!"

John opened his mouth to say
something rude, but Miss Sharma
called out, "On your marks!"

Malina stood ready at the starting-
line. There were twelve children in the
race, but John and Malina were easily

74

the fastest. In front of her, Malina could
see the finishing-tape, stretched tight
and held by the Headmaster and one of
the teachers. Could she get there first?
If only she could . . .

"Get set –"

Malina fixed her eyes on the
finishing-tape. Then suddenly her heart
dropped right down into her trainers.
In the distance she saw her mum
hurrying across the field towards them!
Oh no! Would Mum try to stop the
race?

"GO!" called Miss Sharma.

Thankfully Malina shot away like an arrow from a bow. At the same moment a sharp pain flashed through her ankle. But this time Malina hardly noticed it at all. She sped down the track, ahead of everyone else. She was in front!

But the race wasn't over yet by a long way. Malina's arms and legs moved so fast, they were a blur as she ran. But although she was still in front, the pain in her ankle was getting worse –

"She's winning! She's winning!" screamed Katy.

"She's slowing down!" shouted Charlene. "Oh no! John's catching up with her!"

"Go, Malina, GO!" shrieked Katy at the top of her voice.

Malina was still in front. But her legs weren't working properly. The pain in her ankle was so bad her eyes were swimming with tears. She could hear running footsteps behind her, getting closer. She could feel John Parry breathing down her neck. Any second now he would be level with her. The finishing-tape was coming nearer and nearer – but could she make it?

Malina made a great leap towards the finishing-line with all her might. And at the same moment everything in front of her went dark . . .

Chapter Six

"YOU FAINTED!" said Charlene.

"But did I win?" asked Malina.

Malina was at home again, tucked up in bed. She'd had a good telling-off from Mum, and a good telling-off from Doctor Singh, and probably Miss Sharma was waiting to give her a good telling-off when she got back to school! But no one had told her if she'd won the race or not.

"You won!" said Katy. "You fainted right on the finishing-line!"

"But the race was cancelled," added Charlene. "Everyone was so worried

about you."

"*Terrific!*" said Malina sarcastically. "Really terrific! All that for nothing!"

"Never mind, Malina," said Katy. "Everyone knows you beat John Parry – even if you don't get a gold medal."

"It was close, though," sighed Malina. "I could hear him right behind me at the end."

"When you fainted, he tripped over you and hurt his arm," said Charlene.

"Serves him right!" Malina laughed. "It was his fault I hurt my ankle in the first place."

After the girls had gone, Dad came in to see Malina.

"I suppose you've come to tell me off as well?" sighed Malina.

"Well, it was a silly thing to do," said Dad.

"I know," said Malina. "And I didn't

even get a medal."

"Never mind," Dad said. "Have these instead." And he gave Malina a giant bag of chocolate coins all wrapped up in shiny gold paper.

Malina managed a tiny smile.

"Thanks, Dad."

Dad wagged a finger at her. "And this time you're going to stay in bed until you're better – even if we have to glue you to the sheets!"

It was another week before Malina was able to go back to school. The first person she saw when she walked into the playground was John Parry.

"I suppose you think this is funny?" John said crossly. He had his arm in plaster with a sling round it.

"How did you do that?" asked Malina.

"I broke my arm when I tripped over you at the end of the race!" John snapped.

"Oh," said Malina. "So it was my fault, I suppose?"

"Yes, it was," said John. "And I was just about to beat you, as well."

"Oh no, you weren't!" said Malina. "I won, and you know it."

John went bright red. "Well, I suppose you're pretty fast," he muttered. "For a girl."

"And it *was* you who made me hurt my ankle," Malina reminded him.

"Okay, so now we're quits," said John.

"Okay," Malina agreed. "Here." She gave John one of the chocolate coins Dad had given her. She had to unwrap it for him, because he couldn't use his broken arm.

"Thanks," said John. He held out his broken arm. "You can write something on my plaster if you want to."

Malina looked more closely at John's plaster. There were drawings and messages scribbled all over it.

"Okay," she said. "But there's not much room left. I'll have to write it underneath."

John gave Malina a pen and she knelt down and wrote something on a clean bit of plaster, right underneath his arm.

"I can't see it!" John complained, twisting his head from side to side. "What does it say?"

Charlene and Katy had just come into the playground and Malina turned away and walked towards them.

"I'm not telling you!" she called back. "Go and ask one of your friends!"

"Girls!" said John in disgust.
Malina went over to Charlene and
Katy. They looked at her curiously.

"What *did* you write on John's
plaster, Malina?"

Malina smiled.

"Dear John, See you at Sports Day
next year. Love, Malina."